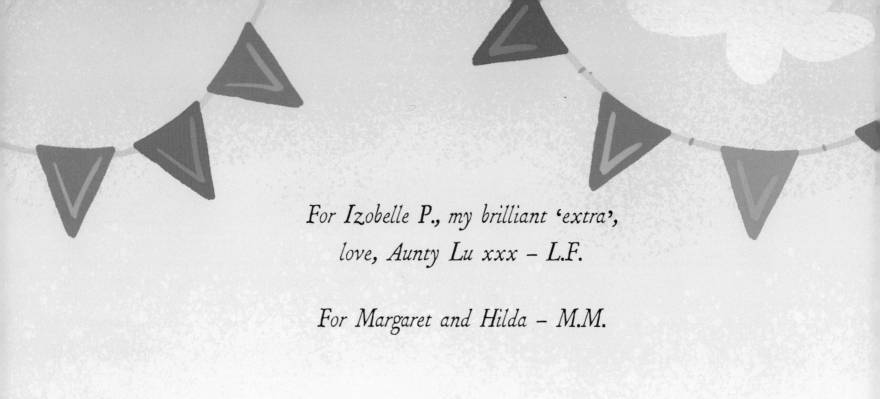

For Izobelle P., my brilliant 'extra',
love, Aunty Lu xxx – L.F.

For Margaret and Hilda – M.M.

BLOOMSBURY CHILDREN'S BOOKS
Bloomsbury Publishing Plc
50 Bedford Square, London, WC1B 3DP, UK
29 Earlsfort Terrace, Dublin 2, Ireland

BLOOMSBURY, BLOOMSBURY CHILDREN'S BOOKS and the Diana logo are trademarks of Bloomsbury Publishing Plc
First published in Great Britain 2021 by Bloomsbury Publishing Plc

Text copyright © Sarah Maclean, 2021
Illustrations copyright © Mark McKinley, 2021

Sarah Maclean and Mark McKinley have asserted their rights under the Copyright, Designs and Patents Act, 1988,
to be identified as the Author and Illustrator of this work

A catalogue record for this book is available from the British Library

ISBN: 978 1 5266 0391 3 (HB) · 978 1 5266 0390 6 (PB) · 978 1 5266 0392 0 (eBook)

2 4 6 8 10 9 7 5 3 1

Cover and text design by Strawberrie Donnelly

Printed and bound in China by Leo Paper Products, Heshan, Guangdong

FSC
www.fsc.org
MIX
Paper from
responsible sources
FSC® C020056

To find out more about our authors and books visit www.bloomsbury.com
and sign up for our newsletters

Lu Fraser   Mark McKinley

THE VIKING WHO LIKED ICING

BLOOMSBURY
CHILDREN'S BOOKS
LONDON OXFORD NEW YORK NEW DELHI SYDNEY

In a faraway land, across chilly seas,
where the north wind goes WOOOO!
in the tall, pointy trees,
two little Vikings were tucked in their hut . . .

Leafling the Brave . . .

and the much smaller
Nut.

Now Nut **loved** his sister . . .

and Leaf **loved** her brother.

But everyone knew they were NOT like each other!

With a sword in her hand,

Leaf could **swing!**

Leaf could **thrust!**

While Nut's sword lay under his bed in the dust.

Leaf was **amazing**
at shooting her bow.

But everyone hid
when Nut had a go!

No, Nut didn't climb hills,

or swim icy lakes,

but the one thing Nut did really well was . . .

Bake ...CAKES!

Yes, Nut's secret passion was slicing and dicing.

And mixing, and whisking, and really pink icing!

From biscuits with sprinkles, to chocolatey cake,

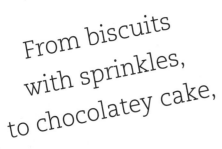

there wasn't a thing that Nut couldn't create!

All day and all night,
Nut did nothing but dream
of sticky, iced buns filled
with strawberry cream.

But early one morning, Nut woke with a start,
as a HORRIBLE feeling stirred deep in his heart.

"VIKING SPORTS DAY!
Oh, no! It's HERE!
The day I DREAD most
in the whole Viking year!"

"Maybe this time,
I'll be **strong**,

I'll be **fast**!

If only, just once,
I could not be so . . .

last."

So clutching a cake in his hand, just in case,
Nut did his best to put on a brave face.
With his shield on his arm,
to the sports field he ran . . .

The Viking horn

BOOMED

and . . .

... SPORTS DAY began!

First was the running – what a disaster!

Though not quite as awful as what followed after . . .

Nut's rowing was worse.

His swimming was rotten. Then . . .

...TWANG!

went his arrow ...

into Erikson's
bottom!

"And now," boomed Chief Olaf, "the Great Horn-Throwing Race! Unscrew your horns and find a big space!"

"What?" squeaked Nut, "but I've nothing to throw – except this pink cake and . . . Oh, no! It's MY go!"

WHOOOOOOSH!

went the cake . . .

"OOOOOOOO

OOoooh!" everyone said . . .

SPLAT! went the cake –

on Chief Olaf's head!

"What's THIS?"
he boomed, and everyone froze,
as a blob of pink icing
rolled down his nose.

Chief Olaf frowned,
then he stuck out his tongue.
He licked the pink icing
and then he cried . . .

"YUM!"

And Leaf, grinning proudly,
held out another.
"These marvellous cakes
were all made by my brother!"

"Nut," Olaf beamed,
"though your throwing's the worst,
at making iced cakes, I think you come . . .

FIRST!"

"And because," Olaf rumbled,
"you're a chef in the making,
at the next Viking banquet
you're in charge of the baking!"

And Nut, at long last,
knew he'd done something right –
that a Viking could bake
and maybe **not** fight.

That you don't need to be
like anyone else.
For **happiness** comes
when you just . . .

... Be yourself.